Fox Friend

by

Michael Morpurgo

Illustrated by Joanna Carey

Contents

To dear Lindsey and Kathryn, fellow
musketeers on our great adventure.

First published in 2005 in Great Britain by
Barrington Stoke Ltd
18 Walker St, Edinburgh, EH3 7LP

www.barringtonstoke.co.uk

First published in a different form by Ward Lock Educational 1979

This edition first published 2012

Copyright © 2005 Michael Morpurgo
Illustrations © Joanna Carey

ISBN: 978-1-78112-086-6

Printed in China by Leo

Chapter 1
Farm Life

Clare had lived all her life on the farm but she'd never seen a fox. She was 12 now. You can live a very long time in the countryside without ever seeing a fox. These days, you're more likely to see one in a town garden or a city street.

Clare's father and mother had a farm which was close to Dartmoor in Devon. They kept sheep, over 300 of them.

All year, summer and winter, the sheep were out on the steep hillsides around the farmhouse. There were three Jersey milking cows and a few hens and geese as well. And Clare had her own horse, Red. She liked to ride him as often as she could. Red was her best friend and meant all the world to her. Clare's happiest times were when she was galloping out over the moors on Red, or grooming him in his stable. Clare spent hours in there. She stroked and talked to him. Clare didn't have any brothers or sisters. But she had Red, and that was good enough for her.

Clare saw her first fox on the way back from school one evening. It was just a bit of good luck. It was cold and it was getting dark when Clare saw the fox. He came trotting through a gate and into the road right in front of her. He didn't seem at all scared. He wasn't even surprised. He lifted his nose and sniffed the air. Then he ran across the road in front of Clare, jumped up onto the grass bank and vanished through the hedge.

"Really lovely he was," she said at supper that evening.

"Lovely? Foxes aren't lovely," her father said. All at once, he looked very angry. "I'm telling you, Clare, the only good fox is a dead fox. We've lost ten lambs this year. Eaten by foxes all of them. And two hens only last week. Foxes are killers. That's what they are, killers."

"They've got to eat," Clare said. She was getting angry now, too.

"Clare only meant that they *look* lovely, didn't you, dear?" said her mum. Clare and her father were always arguing. Her mother was always trying to keep the peace between them. But it wasn't at all easy.

"So does an adder look lovely," Clare's father went on. "So does a tiger. Still killers, aren't they? That lovely fox you saw could have been the one that killed my lambs. A fox is a killer, Clare, and don't you ever forget it. Anyway with a bit of luck that fox of yours won't be around much longer."

"What do you mean?" asked Clare.

"The fox hunt. They're coming tomorrow. They'll be hunting all over the moor. The hounds will soon sniff him out, and that'll be the end of him."

"Well I think fox hunting is just plain cruel," said Clare. "All those horses and hounds chasing after one poor little fox. It's cruel."

"But you have to hunt foxes, Clare," her mother said. She wanted to calm things down. "If you didn't there'd be too many of them."

"There's too many of us," Clare snapped back, "but no one goes around hunting us, do they? It's not right and it's not fair."

"Maybe it isn't fair," her father said. He seemed less angry now. "But that's how it is. One thing you've got to learn, Clare," he went on, "is that life isn't fair. You want it to be. We all do. But it isn't."

Chapter 2
The Rescue

Later that night when Clare groomed Red she told him all about the fox she'd seen, about the hunt, about everything. She always told him everything.

It was March and lambing time on the farm. New lambs were being born every day. Clare's father and mother had to keep checking the flock. They had to find out which sheep would be lambing soon. Sometimes they would help the sheep when they were giving birth. Sometimes the lambs were weak. Clare helped whenever they needed her, at weekends, and sometimes after school. She liked doing it, because it was a good excuse to go on a ride on Red. The sheep were sometimes in fields far away from the farmhouse. And, anyway, Clare loved the lambs.

The next day was Saturday. When Clare woke up that morning all she could think of was the fox she had seen in the road, and the hunt that would be coming after him today.

By breakfast her father had already brought the whole flock back into the barns. Bad weather was on the way, he said. Snow. He didn't want his sheep caught out in the snow. He asked Clare to go up onto the moor and have a last look. He needed to be sure he hadn't left any sheep up there by mistake.

So after breakfast, Clare rode off to look for any lost sheep. As she rode over the hills she could hear the sound of the hunting horn and the yelping of the fox hounds. They were out hunting already. She could see now that the horses had already passed this way. There were hoof prints everywhere, hundreds of them. She was up on the highest hill behind the farm now. From here she could see over all the fields. There were no lost lambs, none that she could see anyway. The skies were grey and heavy all around her. There would be snow soon enough.

She was coming back down the hill when she saw Red's ears pricking up. He'd heard something. Then *she* heard it too. Something was rustling in the bracken beside the path. She stopped to listen. For a moment she could hear only the wind. But Red's ears were still twitching. He was listening to something. He snorted now. He was nervous. Then out of the bracken crawled a young fox cub. He was

so weak he could hardly walk. His coat wasn't red brown like adult foxes. It was grey brown, and matted and wet. His tail hung like a piece of wet rope. And his left ear had been torn. There was blood on the side of his face, and all down his neck. Somehow, some way, he must have got away from the hounds. He looked up at Clare out of great wide eyes.

Clare jumped off Red and bent down. She held out her hand towards the fox cub, very slowly so that he wouldn't be scared of her. "Hello," she said, "You're a brave little fox, aren't you? They can't hurt you any more. I won't let them. Don't worry. I'm not like them. I don't want to kill you. I want to look after you."

The fox cub was too weak to run away. He yelped at her and yapped, and he snarled a little when she stroked him. But he didn't bite. He didn't struggle that much when she picked him up. Clare tucked him inside her

coat to keep him warm. She showed him to Red who snorted again and gave a shake of his head. "You don't need to be scared, Red," she said. "It's just a fox cub."

Clare didn't get back up on Red. He followed along behind her all the way – at a safe distance. And as they walked Clare told Red about her plans. "I've got the perfect place to hide the cub," she said. "I can't tell anyone else, Red. Only you. If I tell Dad, he'd just kill him. I know he would. If I tell Mum, she'll just tell Dad. She tells him everything. So it's just our secret, Red, yours and mine. There's only one place I can think of. No one goes there except me. The old fishing hut down by the river. You know, the place I made my den last summer. It's the perfect place. I'll keep him there. However much he yelps and yaps, no one will hear him. It's miles away from the house, isn't it? He'll be safe there. I can feed him in there and keep him warm and look after him. He'll be fine.

No one will ever find out, will they? Not if I'm careful."

Chapter 3
The Orphan

When they reached the fishing hut, Clare looked around to make sure no one was watching. The door was a bit stiff. She had to kick it open. It was dark inside. But at least it was dry. There were some old sacks in the corner. So she knelt down and put the fox cub down on them. "Listen," she said. "I know it's not very comfy. But you'll be warm in here, and dry. And I'll tidy this place up a bit too. You'll be fine." The cub curled up in the corner. He was watching her as she spoke.

And he was trembling. "I'll clean up that ear of yours. And you'll need food too. Milk, lots of it. You look as if you're starving, you poor thing. I've got to go now. But don't worry, I'll be right back. I promise."

So she left the fox cub safe in the fishing hut, and rode Red back home. It was easy to find what she was looking for. At this time of year there were always orphan lambs that had to be fed by hand, out of a bottle. *What would do for a lamb*, Clare thought, *would do for a fox cub*. She mixed the milk powder with warm water. Not too hot. Not too cold. She had just finished when her mum came into the kitchen.

"Orphan lamb – I found an orphan lamb," Clare said, rushing past her mother. "I've got to hurry. Can't stop, Mum. See you."

She galloped Red all the way back down to the river. She held onto the bottle tightly

with one hand. When she got there the fox cub was yapping inside the fishing hut.

At first, when she tried to feed him, he didn't want to suck and he pulled away.

He didn't seem to understand what to do. She tried to hold him, to show him how to swallow. He got more milk on his nose than in his mouth. He struggled and he snapped. He even tried to bite her. But then he licked his nose to clean it and tasted the milk. He licked again. He liked it. He was looking for more. So Clare dropped some more milk on his nose. He licked it off. Clare pressed the teat of the bottle against his mouth. The mouth opened and at last he began to suck. NOW he had the idea. NOW he could do it. He sucked strongly but he still wasn't very good at it. There was milk all over his face. Soon the bottle was completely empty.

Now Clare cleaned up his torn ear. She saw that more than half his ear was missing. She washed the ear very gently. All the time she went on talking to the fox cub to keep him calm. He let her clean his ear. And all the time he looked up into her eyes.

"I'll get you better," Clare told him. "I'll bring you milk as often as I can. I promise. I'll make you strong again. I'll come back tomorrow. I can't come too often, or they'll start thinking I'm up to something. I'll think of a name for you by then, and get you some more milk."

The fox cub sat on the pile of old sacks and licked his lips. He looked as if he understood every word.

Chapter 4
Larry

At supper that evening Clare could hardly eat a thing. She kept thinking about the fox cub down in the fishing hut. She kept hoping he was all right. "You're not eating," said her mother. "Is something the matter?"

"No," Clare said. Her father came in. He stamped the snow off his boots. "It's a good thing we brought the sheep in off the hills," he said.

"It's blowing a blizzard out there. Never seen snow like it."

All night the blizzard blew and the wind howled around the farmhouse. But that wasn't the reason Clare couldn't sleep. She was looking out of her window watching the snow falling. It was blowing across the farmyard. It was piling up against the barn. And all the time she could think of nothing but the fox cub. Would he be warm enough? Had she fed him enough? Would he still be alive in the morning? She worried for hours and hours, until at last she was so tired she fell asleep.

Clare came downstairs early the next morning. It had stopped snowing outside.

Everywhere was white and silent with snow. Her mother was already up and cooking breakfast. "I've got to feed that orphan lamb," Clare told her. "He'll be really cold." She made up the bottle as quickly as she could, then put on her coat and boots.

"What about your breakfast?" her mother shouted after Clare as she ran out.

"Later, Mum," said Clare. And then she was gone.

She decided to take Red. Clare knew she'd get there faster on Red. And, anyway, she knew how much Red loved riding in the snow. So she got him ready and galloped over the fields to the fishing hut. The bottle was stuffed inside her coat. She had to scoop away the snow before she could open the door of the hut. How pleased the fox cub was to see her! And how pleased was she to see him! He didn't mind at all when she picked him up.

"Larry," said Clare. "Larry, that's what I'll call you. You're an orphan lamb, Larry. Just remember that. You may look a bit foxy. You may have pointy ears, well one pointy ear. You may have a bushy tail. But you're a lamb, you hear me? You'll have to learn to bleat and baa-baa like a proper sheep." The torn ear had not bled any more. "Your ear looks fine," she said. "How come little foxes have such big ears? Maybe they won't look so big when you're a grown-up fox, when the rest of you is bigger. But then, I forgot, you're not a fox at all, are you? You're a lamb. And you're a hungry lamb, aren't you?"

Larry's nose was trying to find the bottle. This time he knew exactly what he had to do. He sucked on it strongly, until the milk was all gone. Even then he wanted to go on sucking. Clare sat down on his sacks. Larry climbed up at once and settled on her lap. Clare could feel he was very thin.

"I'd like to keep you forever, but I can't." she said as she stroked him on the top of his head. His fur was so soft. "What am I going to do with you, Larry?" But Larry had no answers. He was too busy cleaning himself.

Chapter 5
Growing Up

Over the next few weeks Clare fed Larry every day. Sometimes, as he grew stronger she'd feed him twice a day. He was always hungry. No one found out. And she told no one, not even her best friend at school. She told Red of course, but then she told Red all her secrets. Red would listen but he wasn't much help.

"Should I let him go yet, Red?" she asked him again and again. "Would he be OK on his own yet, Red?"

Red would just snort and toss his head or whinny.

Larry's ear was better now. He was fatter and his fur shone. He wanted to play all the time. He'd loved ripping his sacks to bits. Clare and he would play together for hours in the darkness of the hut. She didn't dare take him outside, in case someone saw, in case he ran off.

Winter was over now and it was the spring holidays. Clare was so happy. She could go and see Larry even more often each day. And she needed to because he was getting more and more hungry. But her mum and dad were beginning to ask questions. Most of all when she'd been out all day.

"Where do you get to?" her mum asked.

"Just out riding," Clare replied. "Red needs the exercise."

"Just riding?" She could tell her mum didn't believe her.

"And I go bird watching," Clare said, "It takes time, bird watching does."

"What birds?" her dad asked quickly. Clare gave a shrug.

"All sorts. You know, herons, buzzards, cormorants, kingfishers. All sorts." She saw her mum and dad look at one another. They still didn't believe her. She knew they didn't. She could feel it. She knew that sooner or later they would find out. One of them would see her coming out of the fishing hut maybe. Or they would follow her perhaps. Time was running out.

In her heart of hearts Clare knew Larry was strong enough now to be on his own. For some time now she'd been weaning him off milk. She'd been bringing him less milk, but more solid food instead. Every day now he'd eat meat. He loved meat. Clare gave him any meat she could find, mostly dry meat, but dead mice and a dead bird once. Larry was no longer a cub. He was growing into a fox. His ears no longer looked too big for him. His nose had grown more pointed. His coat had lost its grey. He was big and brown now. His tail was long and bushy. Larry was becoming a fox, a proper fox.

Each time Clare brought him his food or left him, he would scrabble and scratch at the door of the fishing hut. He wanted to get out. He'd always yelp and bark and moan too. And loud, too loud.

Sooner or later someone would hear him. But, in the end, that wasn't why Clare let him go.

Chapter 6
Decision Time

One morning she was riding away from the fishing hut on Red. She could hear Larry. He was scrabbling at the door again and yelping. "It's not right, is it, Red?" Clare said. "He wants to be free. He wants to be wild again. I'm just keeping him prisoner, aren't I? I've got to let him go, haven't I?" She didn't need Red to answer. She knew, and she made up her mind.

She let him go that afternoon. She took a fresh sack with her and rode down to the fishing hut. She fed him for the last time, put him carefully in the sack and carried him out of the hut. In the dark of the sack Larry didn't seem to struggle. All the time, Clare talked to him, as she got up on Red and rode away, up onto the high moor. Her plan was to ride as far away as she could. Then she'd let him go on the moor and just let him try to look after for himself. She hoped he was big enough to hunt now. *He could eat worms*, she thought. *He could catch mice and even rabbits maybe.*

She came to a place in a rocky valley full of trees. It was out of the wind and there was a stream to drink from. There were rabbit droppings all around too. *It would be a good place for Larry*, she thought.

Red drank from the stream as she helped Larry out of the sack. He stood there looking about him, sniffing the air.

"Off you go, Larry," said Clare. "Go on. Go away. Please."

She was crying. She couldn't stop herself. Larry sat down and looked up at her. His good ear was twitching. "I have to leave you, don't you see?" Clare said. "I don't want to, but I have to. You've got to be a fox now, a proper one, not a pet. Go off now." But he wouldn't. In the end she turned away and just left him. As she rode off she didn't dare look back. If she saw him again sitting there, she knew she'd want to go back, pick him up and take him home. She rode hard all the way back to the farm. She just hoped and prayed she'd done the right thing.

All night long she lay awake worrying about the fox. She was up as soon as it was dawn. She had to know, to find out if he was all right. She rode to the wood, to the exact spot where she'd left him. He wasn't there. She called for him again and again. He did not come. She rode all the way down the valley following the stream. He was nowhere to be found. Clare did not know whether to be sad or glad. She was both. She was sad he was gone, but glad at least he wasn't out there, sitting in the open and waiting for her to come.

"Be happy, Larry," she called out. "Be happy!" and she rode home.

Chapter 7
Tragedy

The next day Clare was helping her mother clean out the lambing pens in the barn. It was mucky work, but it made her feel good when it was done. Best of all she liked spreading the fresh straw and watching the sheep and lambs settling down on it.

They had just finished when the sound of a gunshot rang out across the farmyard.

They ran out of the barn. Her father was standing by the hen house. He had a shotgun. "Will you look at that?" he said. At his feet lay a dead fox. "Would you believe it! In broad daylight, too. I spotted him just walking towards the hen house cool as you like, like he owned the place."

"Did he kill any hens?" Clare's mother asked.

"Don't think so," said her father. He crouched down over the dead fox. "Luckily I got him before he got them. Looks like he's a young one. He's had half his ear torn off somehow." Her father was looking at Clare now. "Nothing to be sad about, Clare. Like I told you. The only good fox is a dead fox."

Nethercott House
Iddesleigh
Winkleigh
Devon
EX9 8BG

A Letter from the Author

Dear Reader,

I live in the countryside, in Devon. Even so, I don't see foxes that often. As you know, they're shy animals, and keep clear of human beings if they can. But I do see them sometimes. I saw one once running off across the field with a chicken in its mouth. I saw another curled up on the top of a bank. I thought he was asleep, but he wasn't. He was dead.

I hear them sometimes at night, their sharp barks echoing down the valley. And sometimes the hunt comes clattering down our lane. Once a fox hound got herself lost in our garden, and went to sleep in our garage. She was dreaming of foxes, I expect!

In my mind *Fox Friend* happens on our farm. I could picture it all so easily as I wrote it. I hope you can picture it to as you read it. I hope you enjoy reading it as I much as I loved writing it.

****

Maybe I should tell you a little bit about the farm where I live, because it's not an ordinary farm at all.

Most farms have cows or sheep or pigs or hens or geese or ducks. So does our farm. But our farm has children too, a thousand of them every year. (Not all at once!) They don't come just for a trailer ride and a walk round, they come for a whole week to help run the farm. They become the farm workers! And I mean *workers*. Just so long as it's safe, the children do it. (They don't go into the field with the bull, for instance!)

And it's a *real* farm, not a play farm where you come to cuddle a lamb and stroke a horse, though they do that too.

It's a huge farm too. It's about as big as 250 football pitches. There are 80 milking cows, 500 sheep, 40 pigs, 100 beef cattle, 50 calves, 35 ducks, 42 hens, 3 geese, 3 donkeys, a horse and all the farm cats and dogs you could wish for.

The teachers and children who come all live together in a huge Victorian manor house which becomes their home for a week.

There are dormitories for the children, a playroom (we call it the "noisy room") with ping-pong and table football, a classroom and a "quiet room", a sort of sitting room and library all in one.

Outsde there's a five-acre field to run in, as big as Wembley, with cowpats for goal posts. Nice and squidgy!

Here's what the children do in the mornings with their teachers and the farmers who work on the farm with us.

7 am: Get up. Have a cup of tea. Out on the farm in three working groups (12 in each). One goes to milk the cows. Another goes to feed the pigs and calves. Another feeds the horse and donkeys, and opens up the hens and ducks and geese. Back for breakfast.

9.30 am: Out onto the farm again, one group brushing down the dairy, another feeding or moving sheep, another putting the horse and donkeys out, another cleaning out the stables, feeding the hens and ducks and geese.

11 am: Have a bit of a break and a drink and a biscuit too. (We need it!)

After breaktime, sometimes it's work in the classroom, sometimes it's playtime.

After lunch, we go out onto the farm in our three groups to work again on farm tasks which means anything that needs to be done, depending on what time of year it is, and on the weather.

So we clean out sheds (lots of these), bring in logs for the fires, pick up apples and potatoes (at harvest time), pick raspberries, strawberries (there's a huge walled vegetable garden where we grow our own vegetables) and blackberries from the hedgerows. We help with the corn and harvesting by stacking up the bales for the loader. There is always something to do, I promise you, and something useful too.

We have three good, hot meals a day. (I don't do the cooking, which is lucky for the children!) Supper is at five and then at six o'clock off we go again.

But now the groups change (so that everyone does all the farm jobs at least four times a week). There's the milking to be done, the pigs and calves to be fed, the horse and donkeys to be brought in and groomed, the eggs to be collected, the hens and ducks and geese to be shut up, in case the fox comes. And he does come all too often.

We come back to the house by about 7.30 pm (it's called Nethercott House) for a hot chocolate and a story. I go up once a week to read them a story. And one of my favourites is *Fox Friend*.

If you or your teacher or your mum or dad would like to know more about the farm visits – we call it Farms for City Children – then you can write to me, Michael Morpurgo, at:

Nethercott House
Iddesleigh
Winkleigh
Devon
EX9 8BG

Farms for City Children is a charity with three such farms – one in Wales, one in Gloucestershire and one here in Devon. We now welcome over three thousand primary school children from our towns and cities every year.

Maybe your school would like to come too. I hope so.

All the best,

Michael Morpurgo

Our books are tested
for children and young people by
children and young people.

Thanks to everyone who consulted on
a manuscript for their time and effort in
helping us to make our books better
for our readers.

If you liked this book, why don't you try...

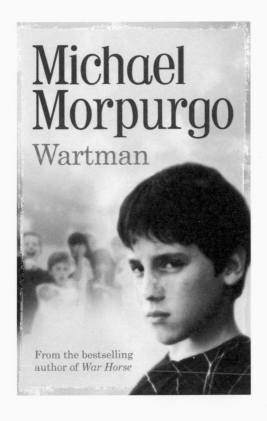

Dilly's life was great till he got a wart on his knee.
Now everyone stares and calls him 'Wartman'.
How can Dilly get rid of the wart and get his life
back on track?